CLASSICS ILLUSTRATED™

presents

THE ADVENTURES OF HUCKLEBERRY FINN

by Mark Twain

 CCS Books

Also available from CCS Books

ROBINSON CRUSOE
ROBIN HOOD
THE 39 STEPS
THE WAR OF THE WORLDS
TWENTY THOUSAND LEAGUES UNDER THE SEA
THE LAST DAYS OF POMPEII
THE TIME MACHINE
A JOURNEY TO THE CENTRE OF THE EARTH
HAMLET
ALICE IN WONDERLAND
OLIVER TWIST
THE INVISIBLE MAN

For a full list of titles, go to www.ccsbooks.com

CLASSICS ILLUSTRATED: THE ADVENTURES OF HUCKLEBERRY FINN
ISBN: 9781910619872

Published by CCS Books
A trading name of Classic Comic Store Ltd.
Unit B, Castle Industrial Park, Pear Tree Lane, Newbury, Berkshire, RG14 2EZ, UK

Email: enquiries@ccsbooks.com
Tel: UK 01635 30890

First CCS Books edition: April 2016

Painted cover: Unknown
Illustrated by: Mike Sekowsky and Frank Giacoia
Adaptation: Unknown
Cover re-origination: Christina Choma
New cover design: Ray Lipscombe
Additional material: Jon Brooks

THE ADVENTURES OF
HUCKLEBERRY FINN

by Mark Twain

IT WAS ROUGH LIVING IN A HOUSE ALL THE TIME, WEARING NEW CLOTHES AND DOING LESSONS, ESPECIALLY SINCE I'D LIVED IN THE WOODS WITH PAP FOR SO LONG. BUT WHEN HE DISAPPEARED, THE WIDOW DOUGLAS, SHE TOOK ME FOR HER SON AND ALLOWED SHE WOULD 'SIVILIZE' ME.

SHE WAS DECENT ENOUGH, BUT HER OLD MAID SISTER, MISS WATSON, KEPT PECKING AT ME.

DON'T SCRUNCH UP LIKE THAT, HUCKLEBERRY FINN! PAY ATTENTION!

I DECLARE, SOMETIMES I THINK YOU'RE LAZY AND NO GOOD LIKE YOUR FATHER.

HUCK'S A POOR LOST LAMB, SISTER. I KNOW HE'S TRYING TO BEHAVE.

ONE NIGHT, WHEN I COULDN'T STAND IT ANY LONGER...

ME-YOW.

ME-YOW.

I SLIPPED TO THE GROUND AND, SURE ENOUGH, THERE WAS TOM SAWYER.

C'MON. THE GANG IS WAITING.

SOON...

NOW. WE'LL START THIS BAND OF ROBBERS AND CALL IT TOM SAWYER'S GANG.

WHAT'S THE LINE OF BUSINESS OF THIS GANG?

NOTHING, ONLY ROBBERY AND MURDER AND CATCHING SPIES AND AMBUSHING CARAVANS – THINGS LIKE THAT.

WE GOT TO TAKE AN OATH NEVER TO TELL ANY OF THE SECRETS OF THE GANG. EVERY GANG THAT'S HIGH-TONED HAS ONE.

WHAT'S THE OATH?

IF ANYONE TELLS THE SECRETS. HE'LL BE KILLED, AND HIS FAMILY, TOO.

WHAT ABOUT HUCK? HE AIN'T GOT NO FAMILY EXCEPT HIS OLD DRUNK FATHER. AND HE AIN'T BEEN AROUND HERE FOR MORE THAN A YEAR.

BET HE AIN'T HEARD YOU GOT $6,000 FROM FINDING SOME STOLEN MONEY.

I RECKON NOT.

THEY WAS GOING TO RULE ME OUT BECAUSE EVERY BOY MUST HAVE A FAMILY OR SOMEBODY TO KILL OR IT WOULDN'T BE FAIR AND SQUARE FOR THE OTHERS. THEN...

HOW ABOUT MISS WATSON? YOU COULD KILL HER.

SHE'LL DO, HUCK. YOU CAN COME IN.

WELL, THREE OR FOUR MONTHS RUN ALONG AFTER THAT. I WENT TO SCHOOL AND COULD MULTIPLY UP TO SIX TIMES SEVEN IS THIRTY-FIVE, AND I DON'T RECKON I COULD GET ANY FURTHER THAN THAT IF I WAS TO LIVE FOREVER. THEN ONE MORNING...

FOOTPRINTS - WITH A CROSS IN THE LEFT BOOT HEEL.

I GOT TO GET ME TO JUDGE THATCHER'S.

THERE...

I WANT YOU TO TAKE ALL THE $6,000 YOU'RE KEEPING FOR ME - FOR A GIFT. I DON'T WANT IT NO MORE.

IS SOMETHING WRONG, HUCK?

JUST TAKE IT. PLEASE DON'T ASK ME NO QUESTIONS.

I THINK I UNDERSTAND. HERE, SIGN THIS PAPER. THAT WILL MAKE YOUR MONEY SAFE – FROM ANYONE.

THAT NIGHT, I WENT HOME FEELING BETTER. I GOT TO MY ROOM, LIT THE CANDLE, AND...

PAP! I KNOWED IT WAS YOU WHEN I SAW THOSE TRACKS.

AIN'T YOU SWEET-SCENTED DANDY, THOUGH? I BET I'LL TAKE SOME OF THOSE FRILLS OUT OF YOU.

THEY SAY YOU'RE RICH. GIT ME THAT $6,000.

I AIN'T GOT THE MONEY. ASK JUDGE THATCHER.

JUDGE THATCHER, EH? I'LL SHOW HIM WHO'S HUCK FINN'S BOSS. YOU COME WITH ME.

PAP TOOK ME FROM MISSOURI UP THE RIVER ABOUT THREE MILES TO THE ILLINOIS SHORE.

I GOT ME AN OLD LOG HUT WITH A GOOD STRONG LOCK ON THE DOOR. YOU'RE STAYIN' WITH ME NOW.

PAP KEPT ME WITH HIM ALL THE TIME. I GOT TO KIND OF LIKE THE LAZY LIFE AGAIN...

EXCEPT WHEN PAP GOT DRUNK AND OUT OF HIS HEAD.

YOU'RE THE ANGEL OF DEATH. I'LL KILL YOU!

PAP - IT'S ME - HUCK!

PRETTY SOON HE WAS ALL TIRED OUT.

I'LL REST A MINUTE AND GET STRONG AGAIN, AND THEN I'LL KILL YOU.

THEN HE DOZED OFF.

IT'S TIME I LIT OUT.

WHEN PAP WENT TO TOWN THE NEXT DAY, I GOT BUSY.

I SAWED A SECTION OF THE LOG OUT – BIG ENOUGH TO LET ME THROUGH.

I WENT ALONG UP THE BANK WITH ONE EYE OUT FOR PAP AND THE OTHER OUT FOR WHAT THE RISE MIGHT FETCH ALONG. THEN...

A DRIFT CANOE! I'M IN LUCK!

I TOOK SUPPLIES FROM THE CABIN.

COFFEE, SUGAR, AMMUNITION, CORN MEAL, BACON, BLANKETS...

THEN...

IF FOLKS THOUGHT I WAS DEAD, THEY'D LEAVE ME ALONE. I'LL FIX IT SO IT LOOKS LIKE ROBBERS BROKE IN THE CABIN, KILLED ME, AND TOOK ALL THE STUFF.

I FIXED UP THE PLACE I CRAWLED OUT OF SO NO ONE WOULD SEE IT. THEN I TOOK AN AXE AND SMASHED IN THE DOOR.

THIS WILL LOOK LIKE THEY DRUG MY BODY TO THE RIVER.

AND THIS WILL LOOK LIKE THEY LIT OUT WITH THE SUPPLIES THIS WAY.

THEN...

I'LL HOLE UP ON JACKSON'S ISLAND FOR A SPELL. NOBODY EVER GOES THERE.

IT SURE IS GREAT TO LIE ON YOUR BACK IN THE MOONLIGHT AND NOT HAVE TO ANSWER TO NOBODY.

JACKSON'S ISLAND STOOD OUT IN THE MIDDLE OF THE MISSISSIPPI RIVER BETWEEN MISSOURI AND ILLINOIS. IT DIDN'T TAKE ME LONG TO GET THERE.

THE NEXT MORNING...

IT WORKED! THEY'RE HUNTING FOR MY BODY. THE CANNON FIRED OVER THE WATER IS SUPPOSED TO MAKE MY CARCASS COME TO THE TOP.

THE FERRYBOAT COME IN PRETTY CLOSE. MOST EVERYBODY WAS ON IT.

THERE'S PAP AND JUDGE THATCHER AND TOM SAWYER AND HIS AUNT POLLY AND THE WIDOW DOUGLAS AND MISS WATSON.

A WHILE LATER...

THEY'RE GIVING UP, NOW. I'M SAFE.

I MADE CAMP AND LAZED ABOUT THE ISLAND FOR THREE DAYS. THEN...

A FRESH CAMPFIRE! SOMEONE'S ON THIS ISLAND WITH ME!

I UNCOCKED MY GUN AND WENT SNEAKING BACK AS FAST AS I COULD.

I DIDN'T SLEEP MUCH THAT NIGHT.

I GOT TO FIND OUT WHO IT IS.

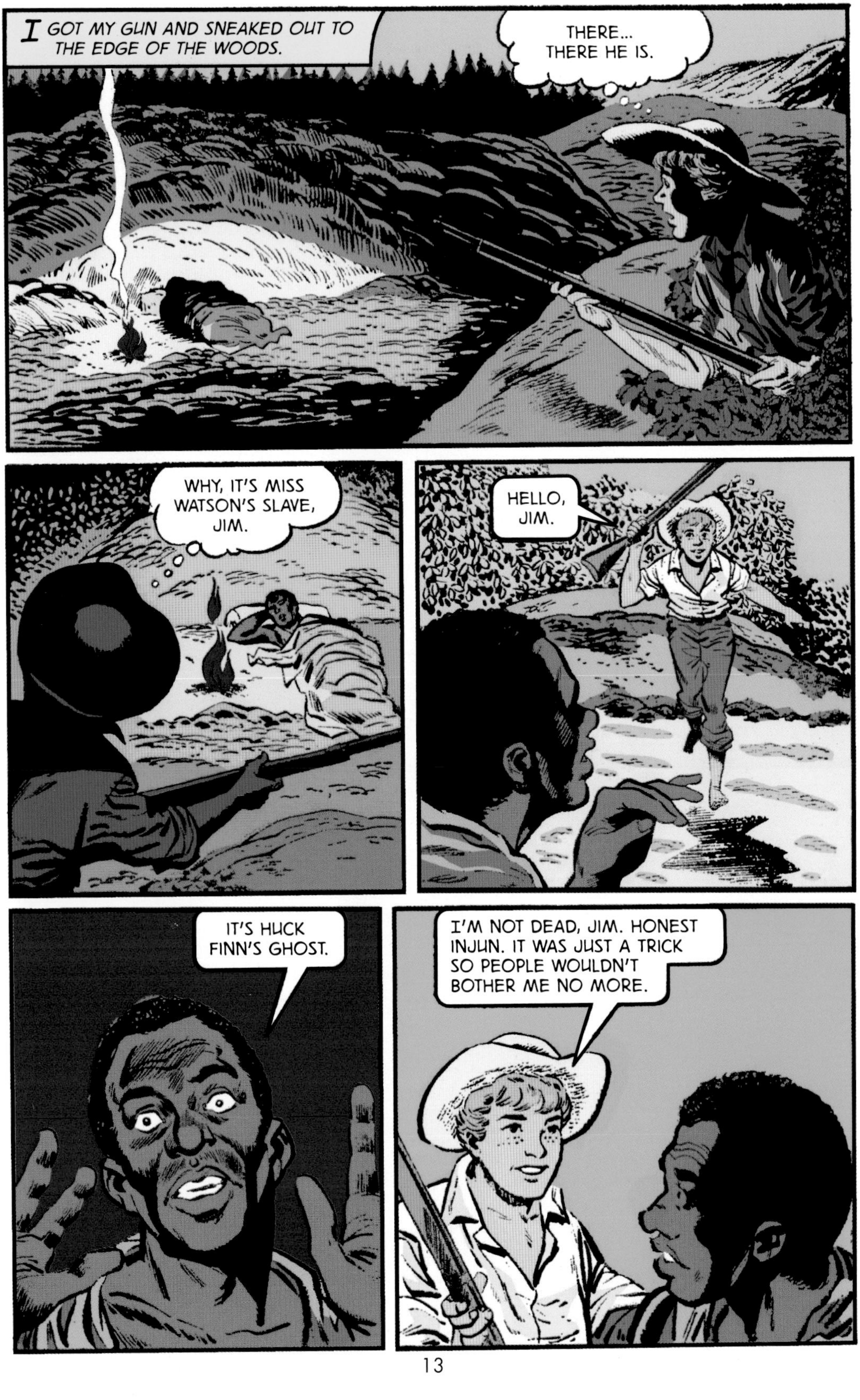
I GOT MY GUN AND SNEAKED OUT TO THE EDGE OF THE WOODS.
THERE... THERE HE IS.
WHY, IT'S MISS WATSON'S SLAVE, JIM.
HELLO, JIM.
IT'S HUCK FINN'S GHOST.
I'M NOT DEAD, JIM. HONEST INJUN. IT WAS JUST A TRICK SO PEOPLE WOULDN'T BOTHER ME NO MORE.

WHAT ARE YOU DOING HERE, JIM?

YOU WOULDN'T TELL ON ME, WOULD YOU, HUCK?

I RUN OFF!

MISS WATSON WAS GOIN' TO SELL ME DOWN TO NEW ORLEANS - SO I LIT OUT.

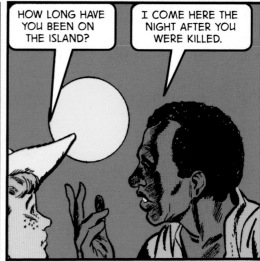

HOW LONG HAVE YOU BEEN ON THE ISLAND?

I COME HERE THE NIGHT AFTER YOU WERE KILLED.

WE DECIDED TO MAKE A GOOD CAMP. WE FOUND A BIG CAVERN IN THE ROCK AND PUT ALL THE THINGS HANDY AT THE BACK OF IT.

GET EVERYTHIN' IN, HUCK. THOSE LITTLE BIRDS FLYIN' THAT WAY SAY IT'S GOING TO RAIN.

IT RAINED LIKE ALL FURY, AND I NEVER SEE THE WIND BLOW SO!

THIS IS NICE. I WOULDN'T WANT TO BE NOWHERE ELSE.

THE RIVER ROSE FOR TEN OR TWELVE DAYS. ONE NIGHT...

CATCH ONTO THAT RAFT, HUCK. MAYBE WE CAN USE IT.

ANOTHER NIGHT WE SAW A HOUSE THAT HAD BEEN CAUGHT UP IN THE FLOOD.

LET'S SEE WHAT'S INSIDE.

LOOK!

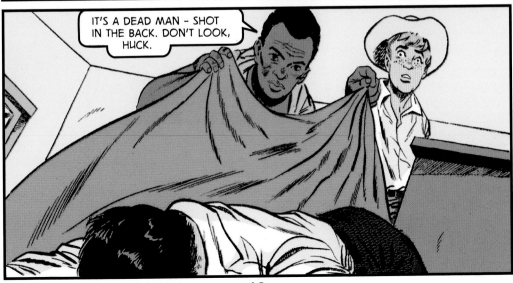

IT'S A DEAD MAN - SHOT IN THE BACK. DON'T LOOK, HUCK.

LET'S TAKE SOME OF THESE CLOTHES AND THINGS. THEY MIGHT COME IN HANDY.

WE GOT HOME ALL SAFE. A FEW DAYS LATER...

THINGS ARE GETTING DULL. I'LL SLIP OVER TO TOWN AND FIND OUT WHAT'S GOING ON.

HERE'S A DRESS AND SUNBONNET WE GOT OFF THE FLOATIN' HOUSE. RECKON YOU'D BE SAFER IF YOU WENT AS A GIRL.

I GOT INTO ONE OF THE CALICO GOWNS.

HOW'S THIS?

IT'S A FAIR FIT...

...BUT QUIT PULLIN' UP YOUR SKIRT TO GET TO YOUR BRITCHES POCKET.

16

THAT NIGHT, IN TOWN...

WHO'S THERE?

SARAH WILLIAMS, MA'AM.

COME IN, CHILD, TAKE OFF YOUR BONNET.

NO, MA'AM. I'LL JUST REST AWHILE AND GO ON.

YOU SHOULDN'T BE OUT ALONE AT NIGHT. I'LL HAVE MY HUSBAND GO ALONG WITH YOU AS SOON AS HE GETS BACK.

HE WENT WITH ANOTHER MAN TO SEE IF THEY COULD BORROW A BOAT. THEY'RE GOING OVER TO JACKSON'S ISLAND TONIGHT TO HUNT FOR A RUNAWAY SLAVE.

HIS NAME'S JIM, AND THEY SAY HE MURDERED HUCK FINN. THERE'S A $300 REWARD OUT FOR HIM.

WHY, HE...

WHAT DID YOU SAY YOUR NAME WAS, HONEY?

ER... MARY WILLIAMS.

I THOUGHT YOU SAID SARAH BEFORE.

YES'M – SARAH MARY WILLIAMS.

COME NOW. IS IT REALLY BILL OR TOM OR BOB?

WELL, ER... GEORGE PETERS, MA'AM.

WELL, TRY TO REMEMBER IT, GEORGE. DON'T TELL ME IT'S ALEXANDER BEFORE YOU GO.

YOU DO A GIRL TOLERABLE POOR. ARE YOU A RUNAWAY 'PRENTICE?

YES'M. I WAS BOUND OUT TO A MEAN OLD FARMER. HE MAY BE AFTER ME. I GOT TO BE ON MY WAY.

ALL RIGHT, SARAH MARY WILLIAMS GEORGE ALEXANDER PETERS. GOOD LUCK.

I DOUBLED ON MY TRACKS AND SLIPPED BACK TO THE CANOE.

I JUMPED IN AND DUG FOR OUR PLACE. THERE...

GET UP, JIM! THEY'RE AFTER US!

WE PUT EVERYTHING WE HAD IN THE WORLD ON OUR RAFT AND SLIPPED DOWN RIVER. THE NEXT DAY...

I RECKON IT'S SAFE TO STOP AND FIX UP THE RAFT SOME.

WE CAN MAKE A WIGWAM TO GET UNDER WHEN IT'S HOT OR RAINY, AND TO KEEP THE THINGS DRY.

LATER...

I JUDGE THAT WE'RE NOT FAR FROM CAIRO, AT THE BOTTOM OF ILLINOIS. WE CAN SELL THE RAFT THERE AND GET ON A STEAMBOAT AND GO UP THE OHIO RIVER AMONG THE FREE STATES.

IT MAKES ME TREMBLY AND FEVERISH ALL OVER TO BE SO NEAR TO FREEDOM.

THEN ONE NIGHT...

THE FOG'S TOO THICK TO RUN IN WITH THIS CURRENT. I'LL MAKE FAST A LINE TO THE SHORE.

BUT I LOST THE LINE. I SHOT OUT INTO THE SOLID FOG AND HADN'T NO MORE IDEA WHICH WAY I WAS GOING THAN A DEAD MAN.

JIM! JIM! WHERE ARE YOU?

I DIDN'T HEAR NOTHING.

I RECKON JIM AND THE RAFT ARE GONE FOREVER. I'LL JUST LIE DOWN HERE IN THE CANOE. I DON'T CARE WHAT HAPPENS TO ME.

WHEN I WAKED UP, THE FOG WAS ALL GONE. DOWNSTREAM, I SEE A BLACK SPECK.

IT'S THE RAFT!

WHEN I GOT TO IT...

HE'S ASLEEP. I'LL PLAY A JOKE ON HIM.

HELLO, JIM. HAVE I BEEN ASLEEP LONG?

HUCK, CHILE, YOU'RE BACK! THANKS TO GOODNESS.

YOU'RE TALKING WILD, JIM. I AIN'T BEEN ANYWHERE.

BUT I LOST YOU IN THE FOG – I REMEMBERS IT JUST AS PLAIN...

YOU MUST'VE BEEN DREAMING.

I AIN'T NEVER HAD A DREAM BEFORE THAT'S TIRED ME LIKE THIS ONE.

AND HOW ABOUT THIS TRASH ON THE RAFT? THAT'S NO DREAM.

WHEN I LOSE YOU, MY HEART WAS MOST BROKE. AND WHEN I FIND YOU, THE TEARS COME. I'M SO THANKFUL, AND ALL YOU WAS THINKIN' ABOUT WAS HOW YOU COULD MAKE A FOOL OF OLD JIM.

HE GOT UP SLOW AND WALKED INTO THE WIGWAM.

JIM, I'M SORRY. IT WAS A MEAN TRICK.

THAT'S ALL RIGHT, HUCK. AIN'T YOU HELPING ME TO CAIRO AND FREEDOM?

WHEN I GETS THERE, I'LL BE SHOUTIN' FOR JOY, AND IT'S ALL ON ACCOUNT OF YOU, HUCK. YOU IS THE BEST FRIEND JIM EVER HAD.

WE KEPT DRIFTING DOWN THE RIVER.

THAT'S CAIRO, HUCK. I JUST KNOWS IT.

I'LL TAKE THE CANOE AND SEE.

I HADN'T GOT FAR WHEN ALONG CAME A SKIFF.

WE'RE HUNTING FOR FIVE SLAVES THAT RUN OFF LAST NIGHT. ANY MEN ON YOUR RAFT?

JUST ONE – MY PAP.

I RECKON WE'LL GO AND SEE FOR OURSELVES.

I WISH YOU WOULD. HE'S SICK AND SO IS MAM AND MARY ANN.

PAP'LL BE MIGHTY GRATEFUL. EVERYBODY ELSE HAS GONE AWAY AND LEFT US.

WHAT'S THE MATTER WITH YOUR FATHER?

CONFOUND IT, I BET HE'S GOT SMALLPOX.

PLEASE HELP US.

KEEP AWAY, BOY. DO YOU WANT TO SPREAD IT ALL OVER?

THEY SHOVED OFF IN A HURRY. BUT I FOUND OUT WE WEREN'T NEAR CAIRO. LATER THAT NIGHT...

IT'S GETTING MIGHTY THICK OUT. I SURE HOPE THAT STEAMBOAT SEES OUR LIGHT.

But she come smashing through the raft.

When I bounced to the top again...

JIM! JIM!

But I didn't get no answer.

I LIT OUT FOR SHORE, WHERE SOME PEOPLE TOOK ME IN. ONE DAY, ONE OF THEIR SLAVES CAME TO SEE ME.

IF YOU COME INTO THE SWAMP, I'LL SHOW YOU SOMETHIN' MIGHTY CURIOUS.

I FOLLOWED HIM AND...

JIM!

THAT'S RIGHT, HUCK!

I GOT HURT A LITTLE, SO I WAS SWIMMIN' FAR BEHIND YOU THAT NIGHT. I WOULDN'T SHOUT FOR FEAR SOMEONE WOULD PICK ME UP. THE SLAVES HERE BEEN TAKIN' CARE OF ME. I BEEN PATCHIN' UP THE RAFT AND WAITIN' FOR YOU.

*A*S SOON AS IT WAS NIGHT, WE SHOVED OFF.

LET HER GO, JIM. HEAD FOR THE BIG WATER. WE'RE ON OUR WAY AGAIN.

A FEW DAYS LATER I WAS PADDLING NEAR SHORE, WHEN...

PLEASE TAKE US ABOARD. THE MEN AND DOGS ARE AFTER US.

C'MON IN.

I LIT OUT FOR THE RAFT AND THEY WERE SAFE. THEN...

WHAT GOT YOU IN TROUBLE?

I'D BEEN SELLING AN ARTICLE TO TAKE THE TARTAR OFF OF TEETH. THE TARTAR CAME OFF ALL RIGHT...

...BUT SO DID THE ENAMEL.

I WAS SLIDING OUT OF TOWN WHEN I MET YOU. WHAT GOT THE DOGS ON YOU?

I BEEN RUNNIN' A LITTLE TEMPERANCE REVIVAL AND DOIN' VERY WELL UNTIL WORD GOT AROUND I WAS DRINKIN' ON THE SLY.

NOBODY SAID ANYTHING FOR A WHILE. THEN...

ALAS!

WHAT'RE YOU ALASSIN' ABOUT?

TO THINK THAT I, A DUKE, SHOULD BE IN SUCH COMPANY.

NO!

YES! I AM THE RIGHTFUL DUKE OF BRIDGEWATER, NOW DEGRADED TO THE COMPANIONSHIP OF FELONS ON A RAFT.

I'M SORRY FOR YOU, BILGEWATER, BUT YOU AIN'T THE ONLY PERSON THAT'S HAD TROUBLES LIKE THAT.

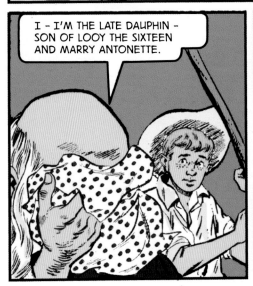

I - I'M THE LATE DAUPHIN - SON OF LOOY THE SIXTEEN AND MARRY ANTONETTE.

AT YOUR AGE? NO! YOU MEAN YOU'RE THE LATE CHARLEMAGNE. YOU MUST BE 600 YEARS OLD, AT THE VERY LEAST.

TROUBLE HAS DONE IT, BILGEWATER. TROUBLE HAS BRUNG THESE GREY HAIRS AND THIS PREMATURE BALDITUDE.

YES, GENTLEMEN, YOU SEE BEFORE YOU THE WANDERIN', EXILED, SUFFERIN', RIGHTFUL KING OF FRANCE.

IT DIDN'T TAKE ME LONG TO MAKE UP MY MIND THAT THESE LIARS WEREN'T NO KINGS NOR DUKES AT ALL, BUT JUST LOW-DOWN HUMBUGS AND FRAUDS. BUT I NEVER LET ON.

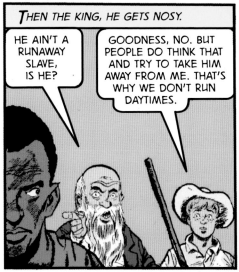

THEN THE KING, HE GETS NOSY.

HE AIN'T A RUNAWAY SLAVE, IS HE?

GOODNESS, NO. BUT PEOPLE DO THINK THAT AND TRY TO TAKE HIM AWAY FROM ME. THAT'S WHY WE DON'T RUN DAYTIMES.

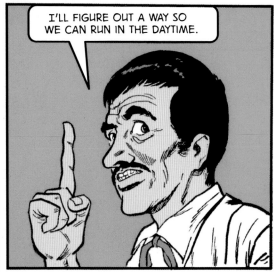

I'LL FIGURE OUT A WAY SO WE CAN RUN IN THE DAYTIME.

THEY DRESSED JIM IN THE DUKE'S KING LEAR OUTFIT.

SICK ARAB BUT HARMLESS WHEN NOT OUT OF HIS HEAD.

THAT SHOULD KEEP PEOPLE AWAY.

THEN THEY STARTED MAKING PLANS.

HAVE YOU EVER TROD THE BOARDS, ROYALTY?

PLAYACTIN'? NO, BUT I'M FOR ANYTHIN' THAT WILL PAY.

THE NEXT TOWN WE COME TO, WE'LL HIRE A HALL AND DO ROMEO AND JULIET. I'LL LEARN YOU THE PART.

LATER...

DON'T YOU THINK MY WHITE WHISKERS IS GOIN' TO LOOK UNCOMMON ODD ON JULIET?

DON'T WORRY, THESE COUNTRY JAKES WON'T EVER THINK OF THAT.

NOW SAY "ROMEO" SOFT AND SWEET. JULIET'S A MERE CHILD OF A GIRL AND SHE DON'T BRAY LIKE A JACKASS.

RO-O-MEO...

WE HIT A TOWN AND PUT ON THE SHOW THAT NIGHT.

TERRIBLE!

LET'S GO!

THESE LUNKHEADS DON'T COME UP TO SHAKESPEARE.

BACK ON THE RAFT, THEY LAID THEIR HEADS TOGETHER AND TALKED LOW. I DON'T LIKE THE LOOK OF IT.

31

A FEW DAYS LATER, THE DUKE AND I WENT ASHORE. A WHILE LATER WE MET THE KING. THEY STARTED TO FIGHT AND I WENT BACK TO THE RAFT.

JIM, WHERE ARE YOU?

THERE WAS NO ANSWER. JIM WAS GONE. I SET DOWN AND CRIED – I JUST COULDN'T HELP IT. PRETTY SOON I WENT BACK ON LAND AND...

HAVE YOU SEEN A STRANGE NEGRO AROUND?

YES. THEY GOT HIM DOWN TO THE PHELPS' PLACE, TWO MILES BELOW HERE. AN OLD FELLER WITH A BEARD TURNED HIM IN FOR A RUNAWAY SLAVE. HE GOT $40 FOR HIM.

I SET OUT FOR THE PHELPS' PLACE. SOON...

IT'S YOU AT LAST AIN'T IT?

I'M SO GLAD TO SEE MY OWN DEAR NEPHEW. HOW'S THE FAMILY? TELL ME ALL ABOUT THEM.

WHY, ER, YOU SEE...

CHILDREN, COME SAY HELLO TO YOUR COUSIN TOM - TOM SAWYER.

I ALMOST SLUMPED THROUGH THE GROUND, I WAS SO SURPRISED TO KNOW WHO I WAS SUPPOSED TO BE. BUT THEN I HEARD A STEAMBOAT WHISTLE.

WHAT IF THE REAL TOM COMES IN ON THE BOAT? I GOT TO HEAD HIM OFF.

I LEFT MY BAG ON THE WHARF. RECKON I'D BETTER TAKE THE WAGON AND GO FETCH IT.

I STARTED DOWN THE ROAD AND, SURE ENOUGH, THERE WAS TOM SAWYER.

YOU LOOK LIKE HUCK FINN, BUT HE WAS MURDERED. ARE - ARE YOU HIS GHOST?

HONEST INJUN, TOM, I AIN'T A GHOST.

WASN'T YOU EVER MURDERED AT ALL?

NO, BUT LISTEN HERE. I'M IN A REAL FIX NOW.

I TOLD HIM THE WHOLE STORY.

...AND JIM IS HERE AND I JUST GOT TO STEAL HIM OUT OF SLAVERY.

I'LL HELP YOU. I'LL LET ON I'M MY BROTHER SID, COME FOR A VISIT, TOO.

SOON...

WE WEREN'T LOOKING FOR YOU, TOO, SID, BUT UNCLE SILAS AND I ARE SURE GLAD TO HAVE YOU.

THAT EVENING...

HE'S TAKING VITTLES IN THE HUT, AND THERE'S A LOCK ON THE DOOR, JIM MUST BE IN THERE.

TOMORROW NIGHT WE CAN FETCH MY RAFT. THEN WE'LL STEAL THE KEY TO THE HUT AND SHOVE OFF DOWN THE RIVER ON THE RAFT WITH JIM. WOULDN'T THAT WORK?

WORK? LIKE RATS A-FIGHTING. BUT IT'S TOO BLAMED SIMPLE. LET'S LOOK AROUND.

THAT HOLE'S BIG ENOUGH FOR JIM TO GET THROUGH IF WE WRENCH OFF THE BOARD.

I SHOULD HOPE WE CAN DO SOMETHING MORE COMPLICATED THAN THAT!

WE GOT TO DO IT IN A WAY THAT WOULD MAKE JIM A FREE MAN, AND MAYBE GET US ALL KILLED BESIDES.

I KNOW! WE'LL DIG HIM OUT WITH CASE KNIVES.

CONFOUND IT, THAT'S FOOLISH TOM.

YES, BUT IT'S THE RIGHT WAY. ONE OF THEM PRISONERS IN A DUNGEON IN FRANCE DUG HIMSELF OUT THAT WAY.

35

IT TOOK HIM THIRTY-SEVEN YEARS — AND HE COME OUT IN CHINA.

JIM DON'T KNOW NOBODY IN CHINA.

BUT IT WEREN'T NO USE TO ARGUE WITH TOM, SO THAT NIGHT WE STARTED.

THIS AIN'T NO THIRTY-SEVEN YEAR JOB. THIS IS A THIRTY-EIGHT YEAR JOB.

WELL, IT AIN'T MORAL AND IT AIN'T RIGHT, BUT I GUESS WE GOT TO DIG HIM OUT WITH PICKS AND LET ON IT'S CASE KNIVES.

NOW YOU'RE TALKING!

IN ABOUT TWO HOURS AND A HALF, THE JOB WAS DONE.

HUCK, CHILE, I'M GLAD TO SEE YOU! AND TOM, TOO!

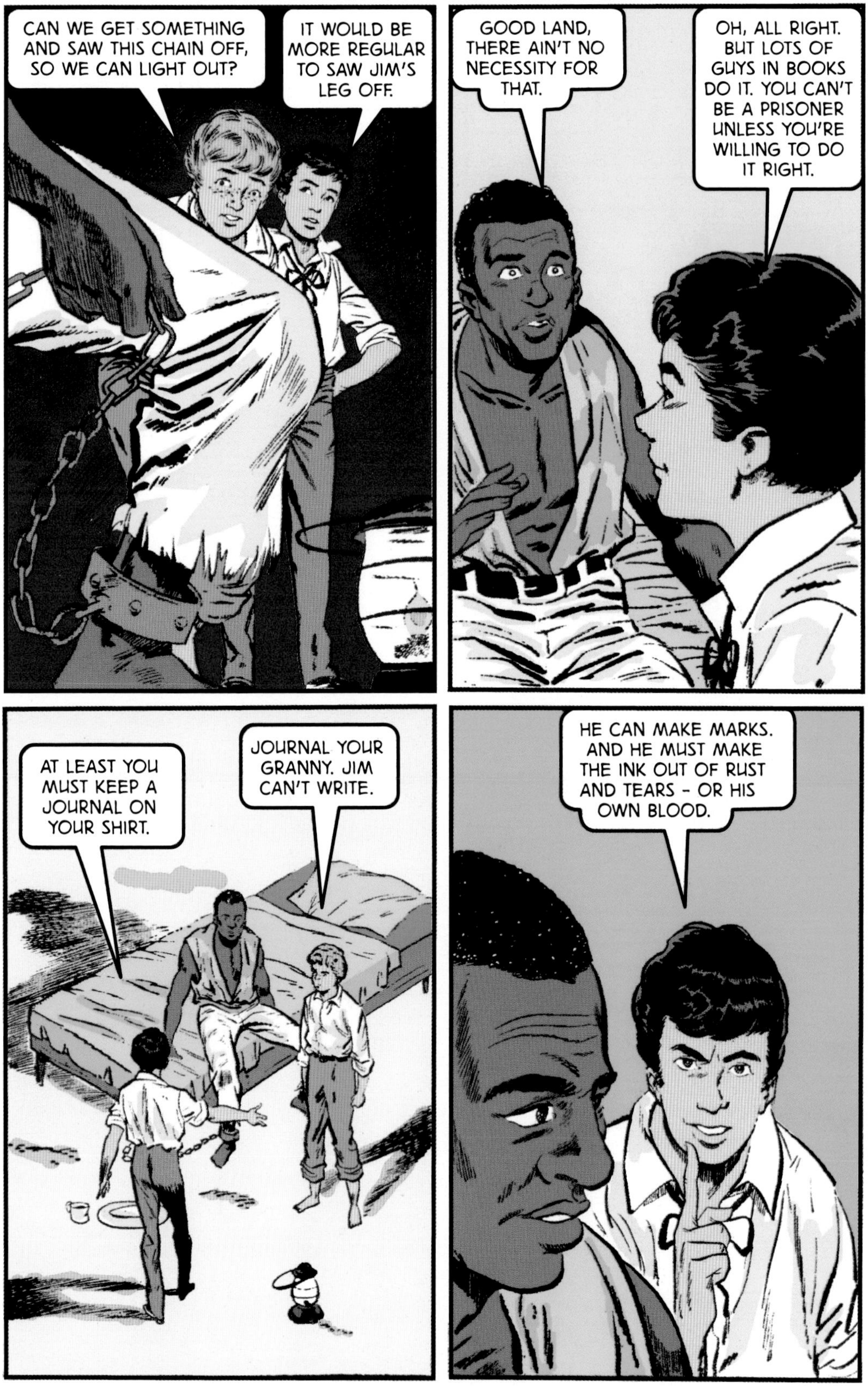
CAN WE GET SOMETHING AND SAW THIS CHAIN OFF, SO WE CAN LIGHT OUT?
IT WOULD BE MORE REGULAR TO SAW JIM'S LEG OFF.
GOOD LAND, THERE AIN'T NO NECESSITY FOR THAT.
OH, ALL RIGHT. BUT LOTS OF GUYS IN BOOKS DO IT. YOU CAN'T BE A PRISONER UNLESS YOU'RE WILLING TO DO IT RIGHT.
AT LEAST YOU MUST KEEP A JOURNAL ON YOUR SHIRT.
JOURNAL YOUR GRANNY. JIM CAN'T WRITE.
HE CAN MAKE MARKS. AND HE MUST MAKE THE INK OUT OF RUST AND TEARS - OR HIS OWN BLOOD.

AND WE GOT TO HAVE A BIG STONE TO SCRATCH AN INSCRIPTION ON – LIKE "HERE A CAPTIVE HEART BUSTED."

THERE'S A GRINDSTONE DOWN BY THE MILL.

WE WENT DOWN TO FETCH IT, BUT...

WE CAN'T DO IT ALONE. WE'LL HAVE TO GET JIM.

WE SLID JIM'S CHAIN OFF THE BED LEG AND TOLD HIM TO COME WITH US.

JIM AND ME LAID INTO THAT GRINDSTONE AND GOT HER BACK TO THE HUT, WHILE TOM SUPERINTENDED. HE COULD OUT-SUPERINTEND ANY BOY I EVER SEE. HE KNOWED HOW TO DO EVERYTHING.

WHEN WE GOT TO THE HUT, WE HELPED JIM FIX HIS CHAIN BACK ON THE BED LEG, THEN...

YOU GOT ANY SPIDERS IN HERE, JIM?

THANK GOODNESS, I AIN'T.

ALL RIGHT. WE'LL GET YOU SOME.

BUT, BLESS YOU, I DON'T WANT NONE. I'D JUST AS SOON HAVE A RATTLESNAKE.

NOW THAT'S A GOOD IDEA. WE'LL GET YOU A RATTLESNAKE, TOO. EVERY PRISONER'S GOT TO HAVE SOME KIND OF PET.

I AIN'T UNREASONABLE, BUT IF YOU FETCH ME A RATTLESNAKE IN HERE, I'M GOIN' TO LEAVE, THAT'S SURE.

WELL, THEN, WE'LL GET YOU SOME GARTER-SNAKES AND YOU CAN TIE BUTTONS TO THEIR TAILS.

I COULD GET ALONG WITHOUT THEM, TOO. I NEVER KNOWED IT WAS SO MUCH BOTHER TO BE A PRISONER.

THE NEXT MORNING...

NOW JIM NEEDS A ROPE LADDER.

WHAT DO WE WANT OF A ROPE LADDER WHEN WE'RE GOING TO SNEAK HIM OUT FROM UNDER THE CABIN?

IT'S IN THE REGULATIONS. ALL PRISONERS GOT TO HAVE A ROPE LADDER. WE'LL SEND IT TO HIM IN A PIE.

FIRST WE HAD TO BORROW A SHEET.

THEN WE TORE IT IN LITTLE STRINGS AND TWISTED THEM INTO A ROPE.

WE GOT ENOUGH HERE FOR FORTY PIES.

WE BAKED THE PIE IN UNCLE SILAS' ANTIQUE BRASS WARMING PAN.

THE PERSON THAT EATS THIS SHOULD FETCH A KEG OF TOOTHPICKS ALONG.

WE PUT THE PIE IN WITH JIM'S VITTLES.

WHAT THEY DOIN' TO ME NOW?

WE VISITED JIM AGAIN THAT NIGHT.

TRY TO RAISE A FLOWER IN HERE. AND WATER IT WITH YOUR TEARS.

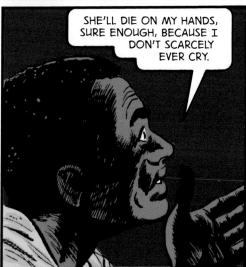

SHE'LL DIE ON MY HANDS, SURE ENOUGH, BECAUSE I DON'T SCARCELY EVER CRY.

DO THE BEST YOU CAN WITH AN ONION.

A FEW DAYS LATER...

WHAT ARE YOU DOING HERE?

WRITING A NONNAMOUS LETTER TO UNCLE SILAS. HE'S GETTING READY TO TURN JIM IN, SO WE HAVE TO ACT FAST. HOW'S THIS?

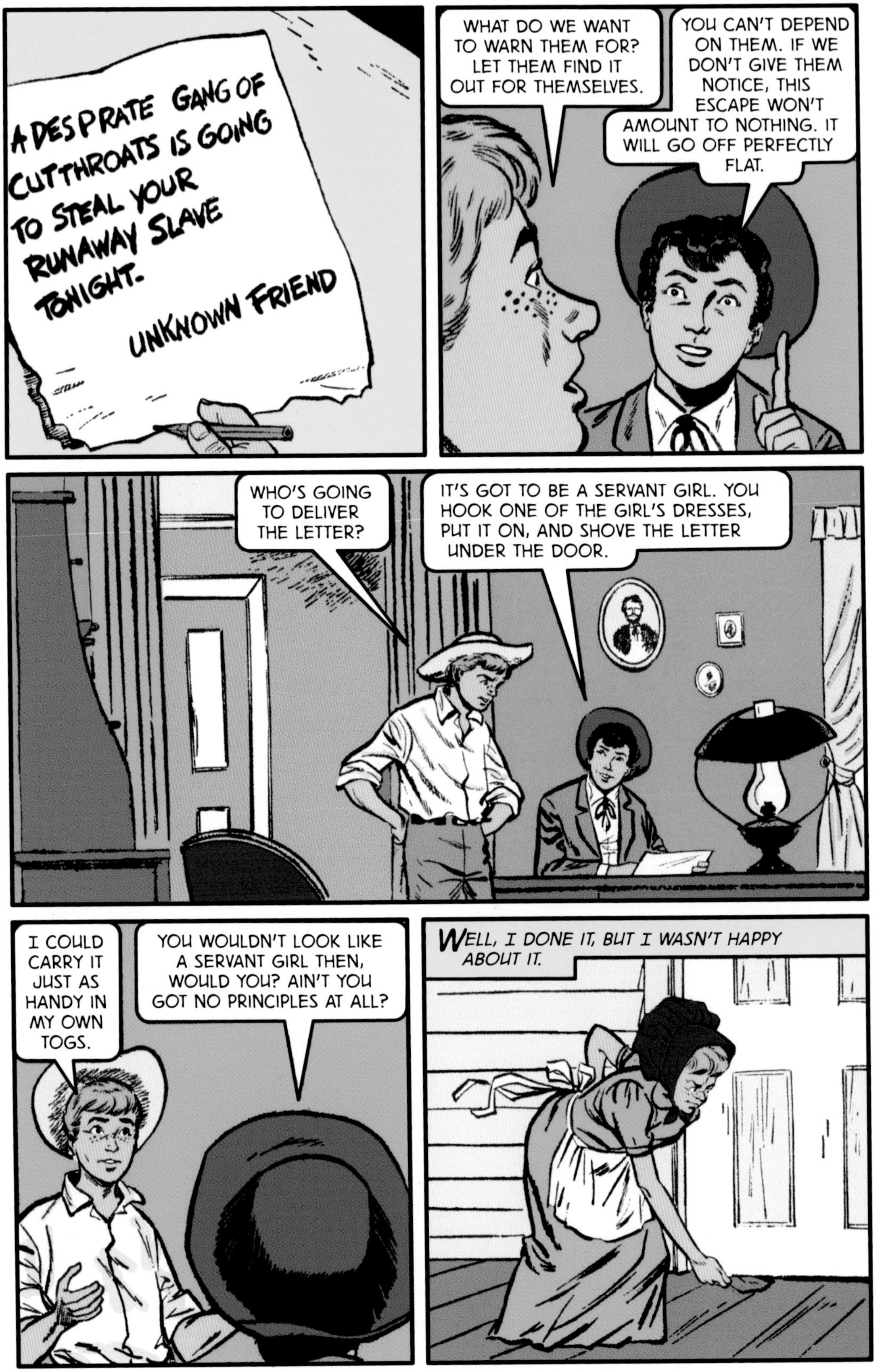
A DESPRATE GANG OF CUTTHROATS IS GOING TO STEAL YOUR RUNAWAY SLAVE TONIGHT.
UNKNOWN FRIEND
WHAT DO WE WANT TO WARN THEM FOR? LET THEM FIND IT OUT FOR THEMSELVES.
YOU CAN'T DEPEND ON THEM. IF WE DON'T GIVE THEM NOTICE, THIS ESCAPE WON'T AMOUNT TO NOTHING. IT WILL GO OFF PERFECTLY FLAT.
WHO'S GOING TO DELIVER THE LETTER?
IT'S GOT TO BE A SERVANT GIRL. YOU HOOK ONE OF THE GIRL'S DRESSES, PUT IT ON, AND SHOVE THE LETTER UNDER THE DOOR.
I COULD CARRY IT JUST AS HANDY IN MY OWN TOGS.
YOU WOULDN'T LOOK LIKE A SERVANT GIRL THEN, WOULD YOU? AIN'T YOU GOT NO PRINCIPLES AT ALL?
WELL, I DONE IT, BUT I WASN'T HAPPY ABOUT IT.

THAT NIGHT...

EVERYTHING ALL SET FOR THE ESCAPE, HUCK?

YES, AS SOON AS I GO DOWN TO THE CELLAR TO SNITCH SOME BUTTER FOR OUR LUNCH. I'LL MEET YOU AT THE HUT.

I HAD JUST GOT THE BUTTER WHEN...

OH, OH. SOMEONE'S COMING.

I CLAPPED THE BUTTER UNDER MY HAT.

THEN...

WHAT ARE YOU DOING HERE THIS TIME OF NIGHT? YOU JUST MARCH UP TO THE SETTING ROOM AND STAY THERE TILL I COME.

MY, BUT THERE WAS A CROWD THERE!

TOM'S NONNAMOUS LETTER WORKED REAL GOOD. HALF THE COUNTY'S HERE TO CATCH US.

BY THE TIME AUNT SALLY CAME UP, I WAS IN A REAL SWEAT.

LAND'S SAKE! THE CHILD'S GOT BRAIN FEVER AND THEY'RE OOZING OUT!

THEN...

BUTTER! WHY DIDN'T YOU TELL ME? NOW CLEAR OFF TO BED.

I RAN FOR THE HUT.

HURRY, HURRY! THE HOUSE IS FULL OF MEN WITH GUNS.

AIN'T IT BULLY!

WE SLIPPED OUT JUST AS THE MEN GOT TO THE HUT.

WE WAS ALL RIGHT UNTIL TOM'S BRITCHES CATCHED ON A SPLINTER WHICH SNAPPED AND MADE A NOISE.

WHO'S THAT? ANSWER, OR I'LL SHOOT!

WE LIT OUT, AND THE BULLETS WHIZZED AROUND US.

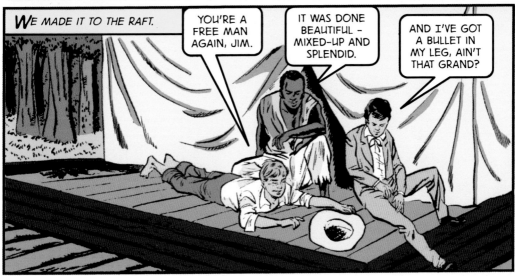

WE MADE IT TO THE RAFT.

YOU'RE A FREE MAN AGAIN, JIM.

IT WAS DONE BEAUTIFUL – MIXED-UP AND SPLENDID.

AND I'VE GOT A BULLET IN MY LEG, AIN'T THAT GRAND?

NOBODY SAID ANYTHING FOR A MINUTE. THEN...

SAY IT, JIM.

I DON'T BUDGE A STEP WITHOUT A DOCTOR FOR TOM.

DON'T BE CRAZY!

NO, JIM'S RIGHT. I'M GOING FOR HELP.

I WOKE UP A DOCTOR AND TOLD HIM WHERE THE RAFT WAS.

YOU WAIT HERE.

I LAID DOWN TO GET SOME SLEEP. WHEN I WAKED UP, IT WAS MORNING. I RAN BACK TO TOWN.

UNCLE SILAS!

WHERE HAVE YOU BEEN?

I SAID THAT ME AND SID WERE OUT LOOKING FOR THE RUNAWAY SLAVE. I LET ON THAT SID WOULD BE HOME SOON. LATER...

SID! HE'S BEEN HURT!

THE MEN WAS PRETTY MAD AT JIM.

LET'S HANG HIM!

THAT'LL TEACH SLAVES NOT TO RUN AWAY!

NOW WAIT A MINUTE.

WHEN I GOT TO THE BOY, I FOUND I COULDN'T CUT THE BULLET OUT WITHOUT HELP. THIS MAN HELPED ME, AND HE WAS RISKING HIS FREEDOM TO DO IT. HE'S A GOOD MAN AND DESERVES KINDER TREATMENT.

LATER, TOM CAME TO.

DID YOU TELL AUNT SALLY HOW WE DID IT – SET JIM FREE?

MERCY SAKES! IT WAS YOU TWO?

BUT HE DIDN'T GET AWAY. HE'S LOCKED IN THE HUT AGAIN.

THEY CAN'T DO THAT! HE'S A FREE MAN! MISS WATSON DIED AND SET HIM FREE IN HER WILL. I DIDN'T LET ON BEFORE BECAUSE I WANTED TO HAVE SOME ADVENTURE OUT OF IT.

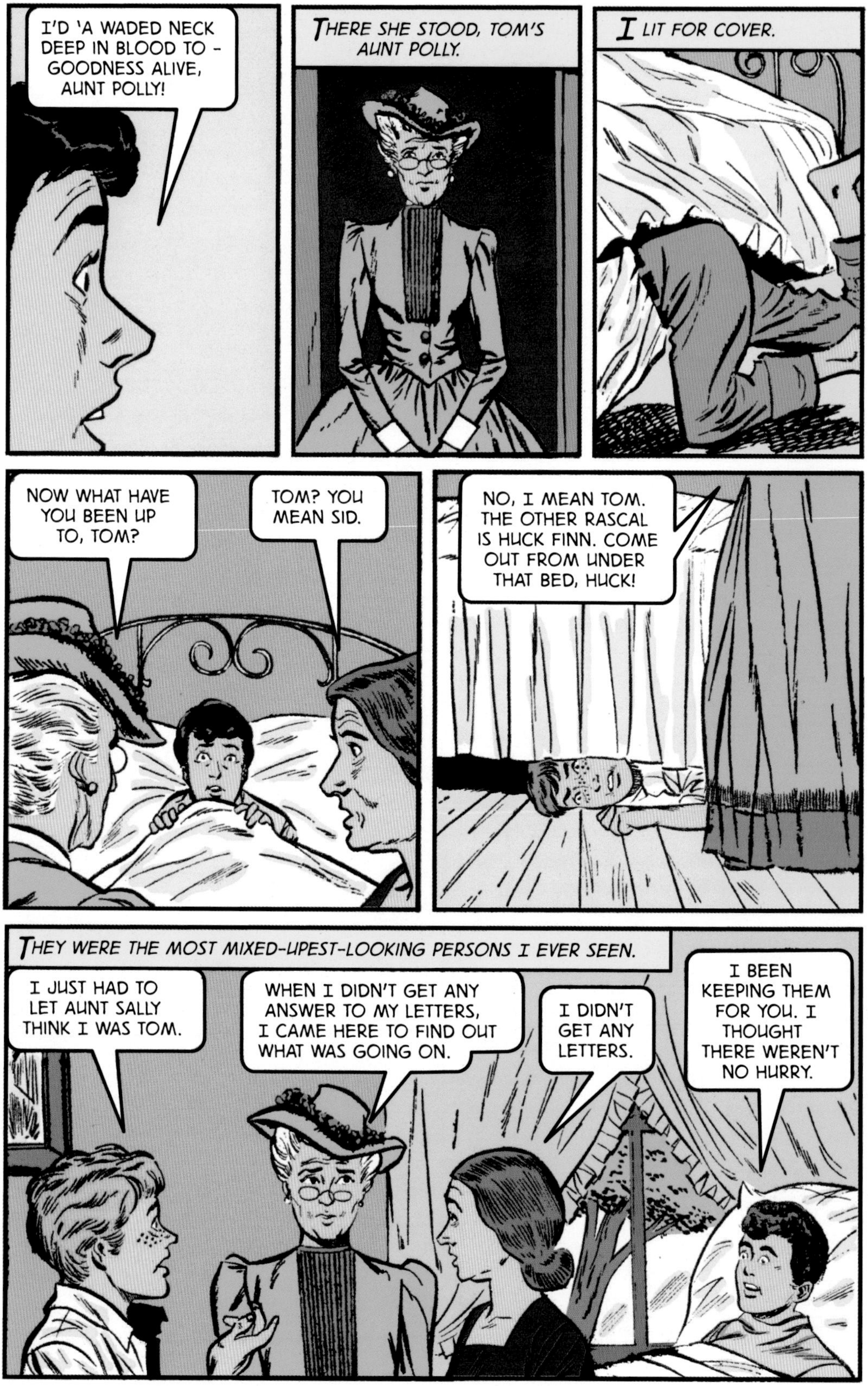
I'D 'A WADED NECK DEEP IN BLOOD TO - GOODNESS ALIVE, AUNT POLLY!
THERE SHE STOOD, TOM'S AUNT POLLY.
I LIT FOR COVER.
NOW WHAT HAVE YOU BEEN UP TO, TOM?
TOM? YOU MEAN SID.
NO, I MEAN TOM. THE OTHER RASCAL IS HUCK FINN. COME OUT FROM UNDER THAT BED, HUCK!
THEY WERE THE MOST MIXED-UPEST-LOOKING PERSONS I EVER SEEN.
I JUST HAD TO LET AUNT SALLY THINK I WAS TOM.
WHEN I DIDN'T GET ANY ANSWER TO MY LETTERS, I CAME HERE TO FIND OUT WHAT WAS GOING ON.
I DIDN'T GET ANY LETTERS.
I BEEN KEEPING THEM FOR YOU. I THOUGHT THERE WEREN'T NO HURRY.

AS SOON AS EVERYTHING WAS EXPLAINED, THEY SET JIM FREE.

HERE'S $40 FOR BEING SUCH A GOOD PRISONER, JIM.

BLESS YOU, I'M RICH.

NOW WE SHOULD ALL GET AN OUTFIT AND GO FOR HOWLING ADVENTURES IN INJUN TERRITORY.

I AIN'T GOT NO MONEY FOR TO BUY AN OUTFIT. I RECKON PAP'S COME BACK AND GOT ALL MY MONEY BY NOW.

HE AIN'T COMIN' BACK NO MORE, HUCK.

REMEMBER THAT DEAD MAN WE SAW IN THE FLOATIN' HOUSE AFTER THE RAINSTORM? THAT WAS YOUR PAP.

THERE AIN'T NOTHING MORE TO WRITE ABOUT. AUNT POLLY IS TAKING TOM BACK HOME AND I RECKON I'LL LIGHT OUT FOR INJUN TERRITORY AHEAD OF THE REST. AUNT SALLY, SHE WANTS TO ADOPT ME AND 'SIVILIZE' ME, AND I CAN'T STAND IT.

I BEEN THERE BEFORE.

THE END

NOW THAT YOU HAVE READ THE CLASSICS ILLUSTRATED EDITION, WHY NOT GO ON TO READ THE ORIGINAL VERSION TO GET THE FULL ENJOYMENT OF THIS CLASSIC WORK?

Mark Twain: A Biography

Samuel Langhorne Clemens, born in 1835, began signing the name Mark Twain to his journalism in February, 1863. He had previously been a Mississippi River steamboat pilot - his childhood ambition - but the Civil War ended his successful four-year run on the river. After briefly fighting for the confederacy, Clemens travelled to Nevada, where he landed a job at the newspaper the *Territorial Enterprise*, and began his career as Mark Twain, a career that soon encompassed not only newspapers, magazines and books, but the stage too, as Mark Twain became the nation's most popular comedian.

Mark Twain wrote *Adventures of Huckleberry Finn* over a period of eight years, starting in 1876, the year he published *The Adventures of Tom Sawyer*. When his friend, Boston editor and writer William Dean Howells, championed *Tom Sawyer*, Twain started on *Huck Finn* as a sequel. He wrote to Howells in 1876 that he had begun another boys' book, "more to be at work than anything else...I like it only tolerably well, as far as I have got, & may possibly pigeonhole or burn the MS when it is done."

He did not burn the manuscript, but he did put it aside, working on it sporadically until 1884. Twain had his first major success in 1865 with his short story *The Celebrated Jumping Frog of Calaveras County*. Some of his other well-known fictional works are *The Prince and the Pauper* (1882) and *A Connecticut Yankee in King Arthur's Court* (1889). His non-fictional travel works include *The Innocents Abroad* (1869) and *Roughing It* (1872), as well as *Is Shakespeare Dead?* (1909). Twain cemented his fame with a series of lecture tours. Mark Twain was a performance, the most successful ongoing show of the post-Civil War American cultural landscape. By the mid-1880s, Samuel Clemens wanted to take full control of Mark Twain's creative enterprises. He wanted to be his own publisher, and to produce his own lecture tour. He hired Charley Webster, his nephew-by-marriage, to run his publishing firm, which he called Charles L. Webster & Company.

Twain's career was not without controversy. *Huckleberry Finn* became a lightning-rod for differing opinion on race-relations. The book was even banned from the Public Library of Concord, Massachusetts. Of this, Clemens wrote "That will sell 25,000 copies for us sure."

Success brought Clemens more opportunities: he published the autobiography of Ulysses S. Grant, General of the Union Army during the War and later President of the United States. Clemens sold more than a quarter of a million copies of the two volume set, which made the Grant family, his publishing firm, and himself a pile of money.

Unfortunately Charley Webster spent the publishing company into debt, and the firm went bust. Bankrupt by the mid-1890s, Clemens had to take Mark Twain on a worldwide tour to repay his creditors. His eldest daughter Susy died while he was on tour and his wife of near thirty years, Olivia, never recovered from the loss, and died in 1904. Mark Twain rebounded after her death for a few years as the white-suited philosopher - the most photographed and most quoted man in the world. He fell ill in 1909, his health succumbing to the 40 cigars he smoked each day. Samuel Langhorne Clemens died on April 21st, 1910.

Discussion Topics

1) *Adventures of Huckleberry Finn* has been banned from schools and libraries regularly since its first publication. What are the arguments for banning it? Do you consider them valid? Is there an age at which someone is too young to read the novel?

2) Crosses, Bibles, prayers and religious gatherings occur frequently in *Huckleberry Finn*. What is the role of religion in the novel?

3) Is the portrait of Jim a fair one? Is it racist? Explain your answer.

4) If Mark Twain wanted to introduce criminals into his narrative, why choose confidence men? Would their function be served as well if they were a pair of pickpockets? Murderers?

5) What becomes of Huck after the close of the novel? Why does he go to the Territory? Is the Territory the best place for him?

6) Who would you rather be: Huck, Tom or Jim? Why?

Timeline

1875 - Hans Christian Andersen dies.

1876 - Alexander Graham Bell is granted a patent for the telephone.

Mark Twain's *The Adventures of Tom Sawyer* is published.

The United States celebrates its centennial.

1877 - Thomas Edison announces his invention of the phonograph.

1878 - Joseph Stalin is born.

1879 - Battle of Isandlwana: the Zulus massacre British troops. At Rorke's Drift, heavily outnumbered British soldiers hold off the Zulus after hours of fighting.

Thomas Edison tests the first practical electric light bulb.

1880 - Wabash, Indiana becomes the first electrically lit city in the world.

1881 - Billy the Kid is shot and killed by Sheriff Pat Garrett.

The Gunfight at the O.K. Corral occurs in Tombstone.

Benjamin Disraeli dies.

1882 - Jesse James is shot and killed by Robert Ford.

Charles Darwin dies.

1883 - Krakatoa volcano erupts; 163 villages are destroyed and 36,380 people are killed.

Karl Marx dies.

1884 - The first edition of the *Oxford English Dictionary* is published.

Mark Twain publishes *The Adventures of Huckleberry Finn*.

1885 - Victor Hugo dies.

1887 - Queen Victoria's Golden Jubilee is celebrated.

1889 - Charlie Chaplin is born.

1892 - Ellis Island begins accepting immigrants to the United States.